DATE DUE

DEMCO 38-297

Flip the book at this corner and watch me roll and tumble

A WORLD OF
TOYS

Written by

DELLA ROWLAND

Illustrated by JANICE FRIED
Border Illustrations by SUMO

A CALICO BOOK
Published by Contemporary Books, Inc.
CHICAGO · NEW YORK

Library of Congress Cataloging-in-Publication Data
Rowland, Della.
A world of toys / written by Della Rowland ; illustrated by Janice
Fried ; border illustrations by SUMO.
p.   cm.
"A Calico book."
Summary: Describes toys from around the world, including a teddy
bear, Chinese kite, and Mexican corn-husk mule.
ISBN 0-8092-4275-3
1. Toys—Juvenile literature.   [1. Toys.]   I. Fried, Janice,
ill.   II. SUMO, ill.   III. Title.
TS2301.T7R85   1989
688.7'2—dc20   89-15738
                                                              CIP
                                                               AC

To José Cruz, who loves toys.
—DR

Published by Contemporary Books, Inc.
180 North Michigan Avenue, Chicago, Illinois 60601
Manufactured in the United States of America
Library of Congress Catalog Card Number: 89-15738
International Standard Book Number: 0-8092-4275-3

Published simultaneously in Canada by Beaverbooks, Ltd.
195 Allstate Parkway, Valleywood Business Park
Markham, Ontario L3R 4T8 Canada

Travel with me around the world,

and we will play with the toys of children from other countries.

Dad told me that teddy bears are named after Teddy Roosevelt, one of America's presidents. This is because he wouldn't kill a baby bear on a hunting trip. Dad still has his old teddy bear, which was stuffed with sawdust. My teddy bear's name is Eddie. When one of Eddie's eyes came off, Dad and I sewed on a button in its place.

I sleep with Eddie every night. Last night I dreamed we went to Florida and went swimming in the ocean. When I have children, I'll give them teddy bears too.

BOOMERANG—Australia

I am an Aborigine (pronounced ab-uh-RIDGE-uh-nee). We were the first people to live in Australia and also the first to make boomerangs. Our special boomerangs are carved and painted with designs that tell old stories about us.

My curved wooden boomerang is my favorite toy. Watch! I can throw it and catch it without ever moving! Whoosh! See it rise and turn around? It seems to stop and hang in the air for a second before it comes back to me. I also have a straight boomerang that doesn't return. It's used for hunting small animals.

I'm going to meet my friends at the billabong. That means water hole. There's lots of space there to throw our boomerangs!

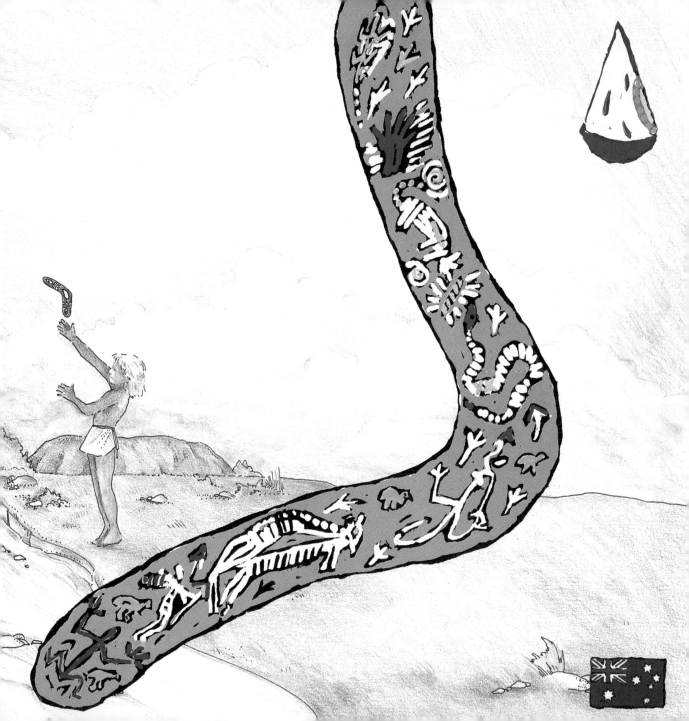

My people, the Hopi Indians, make kachina dolls that look like our spirits of the earth and sky. Kachinas are used to teach children about our religion. There is one for the sun god, one for the god of the rainbow and the Milky Way, and others for the gods of the warm wind and soft rain. There are kachinas for animal spirits and for our ancestors too. Designs, such as a bear paw or an ear of corn, are put on each kachina. The designs tell which spirit the doll represents.

At special ceremonies, the men dress up like kachinas and dance. When I grow up, I'll put on in a big feathered headdress and painted leather mask and dance too.

DARUMA DOLLS—Japan

The daruma doll is named after a very holy man. There is a story that says he sat thinking about God for nine years, until his legs and arms wouldn't work. So he rolled himself around in order to spread his teachings. Daruma dolls don't have any arms or legs, so they roll like the holy man. If you push them down, they roll around until they are straight again. That's because they are heavy at the bottom.

Daruma dolls come in pairs to keep each other company. In Japan, we believe they are special charms that bring health to children.

I made a wishing daruma. I painted one eye on a doll and made a wish. When the daruma gives me my wish, I'll paint the second eye. I wished for a pet cat!

My thunderbolt makes a loud roar when I whirl it above my head, round and round, faster and faster. Here in New Zealand certain priests used to swing thunderbolts to frighten away evil spirits that helped the god of storms. And if the weather was too dry, they whirled them to call the god of rain.

Children everywhere play with wood or metal noisemakers like the magic thunderbolt. These toys have different names all over the world—wolf, monster, howler, hummer, and bull roarer. I guess all children love toys that make noise!

Once a year, we celebrate Kite Day in many parts of China. On that day, the skies are full of huge kites that look like dragons, cats, butterflies, and birds.

A long, long time ago, Chinese soldiers used kites to send messages to each other. They wrote in secret code on a kite, then flew it in the sky, where other soldiers could see it.

When I fly my kite, I feel like I have the sky on a string. Sometimes the wind pulls so hard I think my kite might pick me up and carry me into the air. Then I would ride the wind too!

Many years ago, before there were trains in Mexico, mules were used to haul goods. Once a year, a long line of mules loaded down with wonderful foods and fine cloth traveled from seaports to the capital city. They always arrived on Corpus Christi Day, a special religious holiday.

Today on Corpus Christi Day, we children dress in beautiful old costumes and load little corn-husk mules with flowers, fruit, and tiny toys. Then we join the parade to the church in the city square. Along the way, there are special markets only for children. Bakers make tiny loaves of bread for us to use as money.

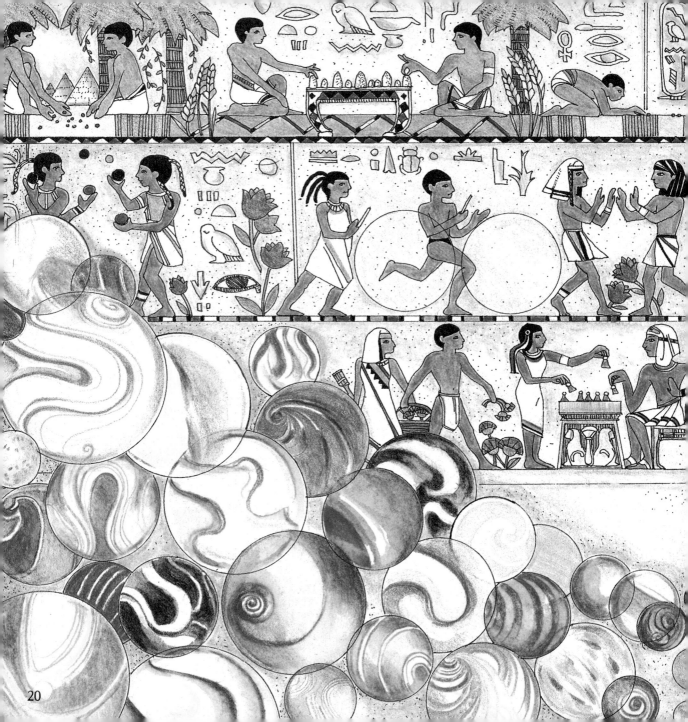

MARBLES—Egypt

I'd rather play marbles than any other game. The oldest marbles were found here in Egypt in a child's tomb. Kids all over the world used to play with marbles made of glass, clay, bones, and even olives and nuts.

My best shooter is an agate. The stone is blue with light gray clouds, and it's perfectly round. My friend's shooter is a glassie with a bright orange swirl inside. We play marbles every day after school.

THUMB PIANO—Uganda

Next to drums, the thumb piano is the most popular musical instrument in Africa. In Uganda, we call the thumb piano a sanza. I made my own sanza. First I found a piece of wood that was just the size of my hand and hollowed it out. Then I attached some thin metal strips called keys. Each key is a different length and makes a different sound. When I hit the keys lightly with my fingers, my thumb piano makes soft, gentle music. It will also make happy rhythm sounds, like my hands clapping and my feet tapping.

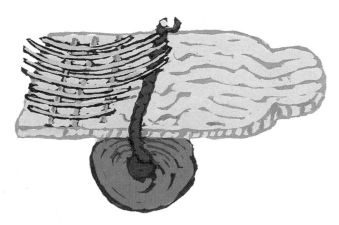

22